SQUAD STRUGGLES

BY JAKE MADDOX

text by Emma Carlson Berne
illustrated by Katie Wood

STONE ARCH BOOKS
a capstone imprint

Jake Maddox Books are published by Stone Arch Books
a Capstone imprint
1710 Roe Crest Drive
North Mankato, Minnesota 56003
www.mycapstone.com

Text and illustrations © 2018 Stone Arch Books

Library of Congress Cataloging-in-Publication data is available on the
Library of Congress website.

978-1-4965-4971-6 (library binding) — 978-1-4965-4973-0 (paperback) —
978-1-4965-4975-4 (eBook PDF)

Summary: Tam is on the cheerleading squad finally. Tam works hard
and she has plenty of talent. But Tam's family is different than the other
squad members' families. There's no way they can afford the cheerleading
sneakers and hair ribbons the rest of the squad has. Several girls on the
squad do things that make it clear that Tam isn't welcome. Will Tam be
able to stand up for herself? And if she does, will anything actually change?

Designer: Sarah Bennett
Production Specialist: Tori Abraham

Artistic Elements: Shutterstock

Printed in Canada.
010382F17

TABLE OF CONTENTS

Chapter One
PRACTICE PREP.................................... **5**

Chapter Two
BREAKING INTO THE SQUAD **12**

Chapter Three
THE NEW FLYER............................... **19**

Chapter Four
THE WRONG RIBBON **27**

Chapter Five
AT THE LOCKERS............................. **30**

Chapter Six
WHERE IS EVERYONE? **35**

Chapter Seven
TEARS AND TEA **41**

Chapter Eight
THE BIG NIGHT................................. **51**

Chapter Nine
TAM SPEAKS UP **56**

Chapter One

PRACTICE PREP

"One, two, three!"

Tam raised her arms and dropped into a split — one leg forward, the other back. Her face in the smeary mirror glowed hot and sweaty. The split wasn't quite right — her back knee was bent.

Tam snapped upright and dropped again. There it was. Arms up straight by the ears, big smile, back leg straight, front toe perfectly pointed.

Tam rolled into a front split, then rose to her knees. "A-T! A-T-T! ATTACK!" she whispered to herself.

After two years of tryouts and one nerve-wracking afternoon of waiting, she was finally in. She had made the freshman cheer squad. And now here she was — twenty minutes until the first practice.

She imagined the blue and white pompoms in her hands. The mangy carpet and water-stained plaster of the bedroom around her faded. Stadium lights whooshed on. The autumn air stung her cheeks as she jumped in unison with the others, shouting together.

"Annnd let's hear it for our Cowwwboyss!" Tam heard the announcer boom. The team ran onto the field as she jumped up and down, waving her pompoms.

"Taaammm!" shouted the announcer.

Tam couldn't understand why he was calling her name. Then the room swam back into focus. Her mother was calling, of course.

"Tam, little bean, your brother needs to be changed!" Ma's voice came from the living room. Tam winced. Now she'd be late. She sighed and opened the bedroom door.

Ma sat at her sewing machine in the cramped living room with its tiny breakfast nook off to the side. She took in sewing for people to make extra money after her shift at the lighting factory.

Tam's youngest brother, Matthew, sat on the floor, his finger in his mouth. Melvin was reading something at the table, as usual, and Isaiah and Adam were whacking each other with long cardboard tubes.

Tam sometimes thought four younger brothers was just a few too many. At least Melvin was old enough to help now. He could do things with Ma now, like go shopping and translate for her. Ma's English wasn't great, so Tam usually did the talking for her when they were out.

Tam swept Matthew into her arms and covered his fat cheeks with kisses. She quickly wiped him off and strapped on a new diaper.

"Ma, I'm going to cheer practice." She waved and ran out before Matthew could start crying. He always hated to see her go.

Tam walk-jogged toward the school. The first practice of the year. And her first practice ever. She was the only new addition to the squad this season. Everyone else had been a cheerleader last year.

At tryouts, Coach told her that fifteen girls had tried out for the spot. And she got it. *She* got it! Tam could still hardly believe it.

Now that she was out of the apartment, her stomach started fluttering with nerves. She wasn't really friends with the other cheerleaders. She wasn't unfriendly with them, but they hung out with different groups than she did. Plus all those girls had been friends since elementary school.

There was something else. It made Tam uncomfortable even to think about it. She pushed the thought aside and glanced down.

That was a mistake, because seeing her bright white sneakers brought the thought right back. The shoes were new, but they were all wrong. She knew they were wrong.

Tam knew they were a big expense, one her family really could not afford. But the sneakers looked so wrong. So cheap, so . . . poor.

The blue gym doors loomed up in front of her. "Welcome to Cowboy Country," the sign above read. This was the same school she attended every day, but now she felt like a brand-new student.

From behind the doors, she could hear the faint cheers and squeaking of sneakers. Practice had started five minutes ago.

This was it. Tam swallowed hard and pushed the door open.

Chapter Two

BREAKING INTO THE SQUAD

Every face turned toward her, like a sea of blank eyes. No one said anything. Tam had never heard silence so loud before.

"Hey, Tam," a voice finally said.

It was Maren, the squad captain. She was very short and very blond. Tam could never tell if Maren was being sarcastic or serious when she spoke.

"We didn't know if you were coming." Maren's voice was loud in the silence.

"Yeah, sorry." Tam said. She wished she didn't sound so out of breath. She gulped some air. "I had to help my mom." She gulped again. "Sorry." She made herself shut up.

"We always try to be on time for our practices," Audra said, a little too sweetly. She was tall with long chestnut hair, the kind you could flip around. "Lateness just isn't a good idea. Okay?" She offered Tam a toothy grin.

The other girls watched these exchanges as if they were at the movies. Tam's hands felt cold. But she pasted what she hoped was a friendly smile on her face. She began nodding intensely. "Oh, of course. I know. I was —"

"Why don't you stand in the back row," Maren broke in smoothly, "next to Lily."

Maren turned and began shouting to the rest of the squad. "Cheer three! Get ready!"

Tam ran to the back row. She hated herself for feeling so scared of these girls. She felt like she should apologize to Lily for standing next to her.

It was a stupid way to feel. She had just as much right to be on the squad as anyone. And Lily didn't seem to care. She gave Tam a real smile.

"Hey!" Lily said. "Cheer three is 'COWBOYS,' three kicks, then splits on the floor, then the A-T! A-T-T! ATTACK!"

"Thanks," Tam whispered back.

Maren tossed blue and white pompoms to the group, and the girls handed them down the rows. Maren faced the squad and clapped her hands.

Tam jumped her legs apart and stood ready. She placed her pompoms on her hips, the same as everyone else.

"Ready? Let's go!" Maren yelled.

The squad shouted together. "Cowboys are the best!" They kicked their right legs high up, stretching toward their shoulders.

Tam snapped her leg up three times. She could almost make her shin touch her chest. Next she slid down into the splits. Finally she raised her pompoms up over her head.

She shouted the cheer as loud as she could, remembering to keep smiling. She lost herself in the joy of moving together with the group. "A-T! A-T-T! ATTACK!" she yelled.

"Nice work, ladies!" said a cheery voice from across the gym.

Tam looked in the direction of the voice and saw Coach Lyons walking toward them.

She was a young woman with a friendly, open face. Her chestnut hair was pulled back into a bouncy ponytail. She looked strong in royal blue shorts and a crisp white polo shirt.

"Sorry I'm late, everyone," she said. "Maren, thanks for running the show." Maren looked at her feet modestly.

"I'll get right to business," Coach said. "Welcome to the first practice of the season. And welcome back to all of you who were on the squad last year. Which is everyone except for Tam."

Coach smiled at Tam. "Welcome, Tam! I'm sure you'll catch on quickly. You certainly showed talent at tryouts!"

Coach looked down at her clipboard. "Now. The first game of the season is coming up, as you all know. I want a really outstanding cheer to open with. Let's get started on a basket toss. I want to work on two groups of bases with two flyers."

A little cheer went up all through the group. Tam guessed that they liked basket tosses. She loved them too. But she'd never done one before.

The flying part of the basket toss was when one cheerleader — the flyer — was thrown up into the air and caught by a group of others — the base. The flyer did some kind of move while she was in the air.

"We need to pick the flyers," Coach said. She scanned the group. Every cheerleader seemed to be holding her breath. "Maren, Audra, Tam. Come up here."

Chapter Three

THE NEW FLYER

Tam squeezed her hands into fists, trying to find her courage, and walked to the front of the group. Everyone was silent, watching her. She shifted her weight uneasily from foot to foot as she stood with Maren and Audra, waiting for directions.

Coach had picked her, the rookie, along with two veterans. What was going on? Was she just trying to be nice? If so, Tam sort of wished Coach would be a little meaner. This niceness was making her nervous.

On the other hand, she loved to cheer and she was dying to try flying for the first time. And Coach had told her at tryouts that she had talent. It might not be a total disaster.

Coach Lyons quickly organized two groups of bases. She paired Audra with one and Maren with one. The flyers used the braced, bent legs of some of the bases as steps. Then they climbed into the basket made of arms the others constructed.

"One, two, three!" the bases yelled. They threw the flyers high into the air. Audra stretched her legs out to the side, though she couldn't touch her toes. Maren reached for her legs, but then shrieked and fell back into the basket.

"That wasn't high enough!" she said, scrambling out of their arms. "Throw me higher, Madelyn! Do it again."

"Hang on, let's give Tam a try," Coach broke in. "Now, Tam, I know you've never flown before, but you're the perfect size for a flyer. And you've got what it takes. I saw your natural ability at tryouts."

Tam gulped and nodded.

"So just go for it, okay?" Coach continued. "The most important thing to remember is to keep your eyes up! Remember, where your eyes go, your body follows. And trust your bases. They won't drop you! Every flyer worries about that."

Tam nodded. She clenched her fists and took a deep breath. Her nervousness faded. Even though she'd never flown before, she could sense how it should be done. She felt it in the fibers of her body.

"Maren, step aside," Coach said. "Make some room for Tam."

Maren narrowed her eyes, but she stepped aside. Tam braced her foot on the strong legs of the bases and hoisted herself into the arm basket. "One, two, three!" the bases yelled, and she felt their elastic strength fling her high into the air.

Soaring, she reached out for her toes and felt them right there. Her arms felt ten miles long. She looked up at the imaginary crowd with a smile and pointed her toes as she sailed back down to the basket.

"Wow!" Tam heard Lily shout.

"Excellent!" Coach Lyons called, applauding. "That was really nice, Tam."

They spent the rest of practice working on the flying routine. "All right, gather around, girls!" Coach called when five minutes were left. The team crowded around her.

Tam wiped her arm across her forehead, catching her breath. Coach made a little note on her clipboard, then stared down at it, tapping her pen on her cheek. "All right. Let's have Audra and Tam as the flyers for the routine."

A little gasp ran through the squad. Joy and anxiety surged through Tam. She wanted to be the flyer. She was happy she was the flyer. But, ooh, Maren was going to be mad.

Actually, she already was mad, as anyone could see by her face. She looked like she wanted to cook Tam for breakfast.

"That's it! See you next practice." Coach Lyons strode out of the gym, the blue doors banging behind her.

The squad broke up, whispering to each other as they stuffed their pompoms into matching blue duffel bags.

Slowly, Tam tucked her pompoms under her arm. She didn't have a duffel — no one had told her to buy one. It hadn't come with her uniform, either.

The others had packed up, but Tam could tell they were lingering near Maren and Audra. Everyone except Lily. She was cramming her sneakers into her duffel bag on one of the bleachers. As Tam watched, she zipped her bag and disappeared into the girls' locker room.

Tam knew why everyone else was hanging around. She wasn't stupid. She knew they were waiting for her to leave so they could all talk about her.

She wished she could stride toward the door like someone who didn't care, but the truth was she did care, so much.

She could feel the whispers building like a wave cresting behind her as she scurried out the door like a scared mouse. As the doors released her into the cool fall air, she knew she should feel proud of how well she had done. But she couldn't get past the thought that they didn't want her.

Chapter Four

THE WRONG RIBBON

Ma made rice porridge for breakfast the next morning. The savory cereal with soy sauce and scallions was the same one she used to eat when she was a girl in Thailand.

The hot rice, along with the bright sunshine streaming through the windows, made Tam feel better. Her brothers hunched over their bowls, shoveling the porridge into their mouths. Tam spooned porridge into Matthew's dribbly mouth while trying to eat her own. Then her phone vibrated.

It was a text from Maren: *Don't forget practice today! Football field, 4:00. Wear new hair ribbons.*

Tam's heart sank. The ribbons Maren was talking about were multi-looped, fancy ones on big silver clips. They cost twenty dollars. She didn't have one, of course. Just like she didn't have a duffel or the right shoes. Cheerleading, she was realizing, was about a lot more than cheering.

Tam suddenly noticed that Ma had turned from the stove and was watching her with that sharp look. "What is it?" Ma asked quietly.

Tam wanted the right hair ribbon so much she almost showed Ma the text. Her mother would buy the ribbon if she asked. Tam was sure of it.

But then Tam glimpsed Melvin's faded backpack, packed and placed by the door. His lunch was beside it, in a paper bag that had been used several times before. It was folded and tied with a neat little piece of hemp string. Ma packed all their lunches that way.

A lump rose in Tam's throat. She tried to swallow past it. "Nothing, Ma," she whispered.

As soon as breakfast was over, she escaped to her room and rummaged through her top dresser drawer. Finally, she found it — a blue ribbon left from Christmas. It was creased and grimy from being in the drawer, and it wasn't on a clip. But at least it was blue. Tam tied it around her ponytail with chilly fingers.

It wouldn't be enough. She knew it.

Chapter Five

AT THE LOCKERS

At school, Tam tried not to notice the other members of the squad staring at her in the hall. The big, bright ribbons stood up from their heads like crowns. Tam felt her own blue ribbon drooping raggedly from her ponytail.

After first period, she went to the bathroom to retie it. In desperation, she tied it around her head with a bow on the top. That looked even worse, but she didn't know what else to do.

She was collecting her books at her locker after lunch when she heard Maren's voice. "Hi, Tam."

She pulled her head out of the locker. Maren, Leigh, Audra, Madelyn, and Lily were standing there, all in their matching jeans and puffy blue ribbons. Maren was smiling. The others were too.

"Hi," Tam said warily.

"Did you see my text this morning?" Maren asked. Her voice was cool and sweet.

"Yes." Tam held her books up against her chest like some kind of shield.

"Oh! I wasn't sure if you had a phone." Maren smiled at the others and everyone giggled, except for Lily. She was looking away toward the bathrooms. Tam thought she looked annoyed.

"I have a phone." Tam wished the bell would ring. She was sweating. This wasn't a friendly visit, that much was clear.

"But not a hair ribbon, right?" Maren laughed again.

"What? I have a ribbon." Tam's hand crept up to feel the grubby ribbon tied around her head. She knew where this conversation was going, but like a mouse squeezed by a snake, she couldn't seem to find a way out.

"Oh! That. I see. That's your ribbon. Aw. How cute." Maren's voice had grown dangerously soft.

She stepped closer. Her breath smelled like mint candy. The others closed in behind her. Lily hung back. Tam backed up until she felt the cold metal of the locker door pressing against her back.

"Here." Maren dangled something, as if she were holding a mouse by the tail. It was a twenty-dollar bill.

"You probably need this, right?" Maren asked. "You know, for the right hair ribbon." She swung the bill back and forth, as if it would hypnotize Tam. Over Maren's shoulder, Tam could see Lily, looking upset.

Rage and shame choked Tam. She wanted to swat that stupid bill right into Maren's sweet, smiling, bland face.

She turned back to her locker instead and stared into it. She stayed that way until she heard footsteps going away from her, back down the hall. A faint, tinkling laugh floated back to her.

Tam closed her eyes and rested her forehead on the cool metal of the locker. She wished she could stay that way forever.

Chapter Six

WHERE IS EVERYONE?

After four periods, including algebra, American history, biology, and choir, Tam had finally shoved the money incident into the back of her mind.

In spite of everything, her spirits rose as she ran onto the football field after the last bell. She'd worn leggings and a T-shirt today, so she didn't have to change. Her pompoms were safely in her backpack. She didn't want to risk being late again.

The sky was that blue you only get in the autumn and the trees shook their gaudy fall tresses in the light breeze. Red, orange, shocking pink, mauve, and silver nearly exploded against the peaceful sky. The football field stretched jewel-green against the crisp white lines and blue bleachers.

She was five minutes early — that was good. And she was the first one. Tam dropped her backpack by the team bench and did a few lunges and toe-touches to warm up. Still, no one arrived.

She looked at her phone. It was 4:05. They were probably changing. She jogged the length of the track — one-eighth of a mile — then silently ran through the ATTACK cheer, mouthing the words.

She could almost forget all the icky stuff of these last couple of days when she was out here, jumping, doing the cheers. She pictured the bleachers packed with people against a frosty black sky, and herself under the lights. The thought of it made her shiver with excitement. Tomorrow! That was all happening tomorrow!

Where were they? Tam looked at her phone again — 4:15. Still no one. Wait, did she get the day wrong? Tam clicked back through her messages. No, here it was — *Don't forget practice today! Football field, 4:00.* She felt her excitement draining away. Something was up. She didn't know what, but it couldn't be good.

Her hands clammy again, Tam stuffed her pompoms into her backpack and slung it onto her shoulders. She didn't know what else to do. She might as well go home.

Tam trudged up the asphalt path toward the school and pushed through the gate. The gym doors were just ahead. But as Tam passed them, she heard the unmistakable sounds of cheers and jumps from inside.

The bottom fell out of her stomach. She felt sick and wished she could run away. Instead, she crept up to the doors and eased one open. She pressed her eye to the crack.

There they were — all in their practice clothes and pompoms. Audra was shouting something at everyone with her hands on her hips. Coach sat on one of the bleachers, watching intently. No one noticed Tam.

She stood outside a long time, clenching and unclenching her fists. Her throat felt swollen and rough, as if she were breathing past sandpaper. At last, she walked slowly away from the school across the parking lot.

The girls had done this to leave her out, obviously. To hurt her. Just to be mean. Because she was poor and gross. Tam looked down at the stiff, cheap sneakers, still so blindingly white, still so wrong. She was so filled with rage, she wanted to rip them off and fling them into the street.

That's it, Tam thought. *I can't do it. I thought I could but I can't. No one wants me. They all hate me. So I'll quit. I'll quit and they can have everything back the way it was before dumb, gross Tam started messing everything up.*

So that was that. Her mind was made up. And the game was over — before it had really even begun.

Chapter Seven

TEARS AND TEA

Tam barely heard Ma call her name as she slammed into the house. She ignored Melvin and Isaiah in the living room and ran straight into her own room. She ripped off her sneakers and threw them against the wall, then flung herself onto the bed.

She buried her face in her familiar old pillow with its faded, pink-flowered pillowcase. There, she finally let the hot tears run down the sides of her face. All the tryouts, all that work — for nothing. She'd never fly into the night sky under those lights. It was over.

"Tam?" Ma knocked at the door, then opened it. "What's wrong, Little Bean?"

"Nothing, Ma. Please, I want to be alone." Tam kept her face in the pillow.

She felt her mother sit down on the bed. Her calloused hand rubbed Tam's back up and down, side to side. Tam sighed. Her mother used to make everything better with that backrub. Not anymore.

"Is something wrong with your cheers?" Ma asked.

Tam peeked her face out from the pillow and looked at her mother, with her black hair neatly smoothed back into her braid and her worn face creased with concern.

She thought about lying, but Ma would know. She always did. Tam nodded. "Yeah. Something like that."

Ma looked at Tam a long time, then her gaze traveled around the room until it found the sneakers, lying where they had landed on top of the dresser. She looked at the sneakers a long time, then back at Tam.

Then she nodded and gave Tam a brisk pat on the rump, just as the doorbell rang. "You rest for a bit, then I'll bring you special tea, okay?"

Ma's special tea — strong, with milk and sugar — was one of her standard remedies. And it often worked. Tam wasn't sure about today, though.

A tangle of voices rose from the living room and dully, Tam wondered who it was. She didn't really care, though. Probably a neighbor.

"I will make tea," Tam heard Ma say, and her footsteps tapped away toward the kitchen.

A moment later, the door creaked. "Tam?" a hesitant voice asked.

Tam sat straight up. It was Lily. "Hey!" she said, swiping at her hair. It seemed to be standing entirely on end. She scrubbed at her cheeks with the back of her hand.

Timidly, Lily closed the door behind her. "Hi." She perched on the edge of the bed.

Tam anxiously looked around the room. It looked worse than ever. The carpet was gray and dingy, and the plaster was cracked all down one wall. The paint was peeling away from her dresser and desk, and the old lampshade by her bed was torn. What would Lily think of this place?

Before either of them could say anything, Ma rattled through the door with a tray. "Tea!" she sang as Matthew tumbled around her feet. "Here you go, girls." She set down the tray, which held a black teapot, two matching cups with saucers, a pitcher with cream, a sugar bowl, and two spoons.

"Me tea!" Matthew crowed, trying to reach the tray.

"No you tea," Ma told him, whisking him out of the way. "This is for the girls."

"Thanks, Mrs. Aromdee," Lily said. "That's a really pretty teapot."

Tam looked at her in surprise. She didn't know Lily knew her last name.

"Yeah, thanks, Ma," she managed. Tam watched as her mother carried Matthew out of the room, softly closing the door behind her. Ma could be pretty great sometimes.

"Listen," Lily said as soon as the door closed. "I wanted to tell you I'm sorry about this afternoon. Maren sent you a text with the wrong place so you couldn't find us. And she wanted us to learn a new move so you wouldn't know and then you'd be embarrassed at the game."

Tam nodded as she poured tea into each of the cups.

"But that's not really what I'm sorry for," Lily went on. "I'm really sorry for not standing up to her before now. I was just going along, hoping things would get better, and that was wrong. I told Maren she was wrong this afternoon. But I wanted to apologize to you too."

Lily finished all in a rush, her cheeks flaming pink. She stared hard at Tam's bedspread, picking at a little thread there.

Tam sat still, trying to absorb Lily's words. She realized her mouth was hanging open a little and quickly closed it. "Oh. I, um . . . thanks."

She felt so odd — all churned up and angry about stupid Maren and the others, but so nervously grateful to Lily that she thought she might cry.

Lily stood up from the bed. "Let's work on the new move. It's right before we get into position for the toss. You do the toe-touch jump, then the new part is a back handspring, then down on one knee, then the toss."

Tam stood beside Lily, looking at their reflections in the big mirror over her dresser. They stood feet apart, hands on their hips. "Ready? Let's go!" Lily said.

Tam's room gave them just enough space to practice if they took turns. Lily went first. Tam watched her, then got ready to try it. She reached for her toes, then flipped backward into a handspring. Tam felt that snap of her lower body flipping over. It was a feeling that always told her the move was going right. She landed, thudding on the floor, then dropped to one knee. She held her arms overhead, holding imaginary pompoms, a big smile on her face.

Tam looked at her reflection in the mirror. "I think I get it," she said. "I'll go over it some more tonight."

Lily hauled Tam to her feet. "Maren will be so surprised tomorrow."

Tam couldn't help smiling. "The cheering will be the best part," she said. "But that will be second best."

Chapter Eight

THE BIG NIGHT

"And give it up for our Cowwbooysss!"
The announcer's voice boomed into the
crisp black night.

The big stadium lights bathed everything
in an unearthly bright white. The wind
whipped the flags flying above the packed
bleachers. The field and the track glowed
vivid green and white. Ma and the boys
were in that crowd somewhere. It was just
as Tam had always dreamed.

She jumped and kicked her legs with the others, cheering as loudly as she could. The team, glittering in their blue and white uniforms, ran onto the field.

They can't leave me out, Tam thought. *I'm here to stay.*

She was glad Lily had her back. She'd do the routine they thought she didn't know, and she'd show them once and for all.

"First cheer!" Maren called.

"Where's Coach?" Tam muttered to Lily, scanning the sidelines.

"She had to miss at the last minute. Her little boy got sick. She put Maren in charge." Lily looked worried.

Tam gulped. Maren in charge. A warning bell clanged in her head. But there was no time to think further. This was it.

They lined up, facing the crowd, hands on their hips, feet apart. Lily stood next to Tam. She could feel the support radiating from her friend. It made her feel even stronger.

"Ready? Let's go!" Maren yelled.

Tam launched herself into the toe-touch with everyone else. She flipped into the back handspring. The crowd cheered.

Tam didn't look around, and she didn't stop. She could feel the confusion among the rest of the squad. They dropped down onto one knee.

Tam snuck a glance at Maren as she shook her pompoms over her head. Maren's face was white with anger. Her lips were a thin, hard line. Tam caught her gaze, and Maren narrowed her eyes.

It was time for the basket toss. Moving seamlessly, the squad broke into their two groups. One group of bases stood ready for Audra. Tam moved into the ready position in front of her group of bases. The girls braced their legs and linked their arms.

Suddenly, Tam felt someone push her hard, and she staggered to the side. It was Leigh. She didn't look at Tam — she just returned to her place as a base. Before Tam could recover, Maren slid into the flyer position.

Chapter Nine

TAM SPEAKS UP

"One, two, three!" Leigh yelled. Before Tam could even think, the bases flung the flyers into the air. Tam stood awkwardly between the two groups. She felt the eyes of the crowd on her as she fought back tears.

The rest of the cheer — the rest of the night — was a blur. Tam's body did the cheers, but she couldn't keep the mask of sadness from her face.

Finally, the Cowboys wrapped up the game, 24–14. Happy fans streamed from the stands. Tam couldn't stand to talk to anyone. She knew her family would be waiting for her outside the locker room. She couldn't bear to see them.

Tam walked up the path to the gym and continued through to the locker room. The girls were chattering as she came in, but they quickly stopped.

"Oh! Tam! Sorry about the toss. It was just a last-minute thing. You understand." Maren's voice was sleek and confident.

So that's how it would go. Tam was supposed to just accept her lame explanation and everything would go on — the Maren way.

Before she could help herself, Tam nodded. She felt clogged. She couldn't do anything. She couldn't say anything.

Numbly, she sat down on the bench as Maren gave her a self-satisfied little smile, then turned back to her own locker.

Lily sat down and nudged Tam. She looked up. *Say something!* Lily mouthed. Tam just looked at her. "Come on!" Lily whispered. "I'll back you up!"

Tam looked at her friend, so strong beside her. She thought of Ma and the four eager little boys, all waiting for her outside the door. Something bubbled up in her.

"Maren!" she barked, jumping up.

Maren turned around so quickly, she banged her head on her locker door. "What?" she rubbed her head.

"I was shoved out of the way." Tam could hardly believe that the aggressive voice echoing around the room was hers.

"You changed the practice and tried to shut me out of the routine." She went on. "All I've wanted is to cheer on this squad, and you've treated me badly from the start — all because I don't have a lot of money, or the right shoes, or a new hair ribbon." She took a breath, then continued, "But I know what's really been bothering you."

Maren stared at her, eyes bulging, mouth hanging open. The room was utterly silent.

"You just can't stand that I'm a better cheerleader than you. You just hate that some weird, poor girl can knock you out of your spot." Tam's voice was soft. She didn't need to shout. Maren heard her words. She could tell.

Several girls gasped behind her, but Tam didn't look around. She gathered up her pompoms.

Lily zipped her duffel with a flourish. "Come on, Tam," she said loudly. She linked elbows with Tam. "Let's go. Do you think your mom will make us more of that tea?"

Tam grinned. "I bet she just might." She turned to the rest of the room. Everyone was staring as if she was a zoo exhibit. "See you all at practice on Monday."

Together, Tam and Lily marched out of the locker room and through the gym. Ma and the boys were waiting outside the blue doors, just as she knew they'd be.

"Tam! Tam!" they all crowed as if she was a celebrity. Melvin high-fived her as Matthew jumped at her feet, demanding to be picked up.

Tam swept Matthew into her arms as Isaiah and Adam crowded up against her. Ma hugged her and smoothed her hair.

"That was wonderful cheering, Little Bean. You too, Lily," Ma said, beaming at them both. "But what happened at the beginning?"

Tam rolled her eyes at Lily. "Nothing, Ma. Nothing I can't take care of."

Nothing I can't take care of now, Tam thought. It felt good to speak up — especially with a friend by her side. She'd remember that from now on.

And she'd start on Monday.

Author Bio

Emma Carlson Berne has written over eighty books for children and young adults. She especially loves writing about sports, history, and the outdoors. When she's not writing books, Emma rides horses, runs after her three little boys, and walks in the woods near her home in Cincinnati, Ohio.

Illustrator Bio

Katie Wood fell in love with drawing when she was very small. Since graduating from Loughborough University School of Art and Design in 2004, she has been living her dream working as a freelance illustrator. From her studio in Leicester, England, she creates bright and lively illustrations for books and magazines all over the world.

Glossary

ability (uh-BILL-uh-tee) — having the skill to do something

aggressive (uh-GREH-siv) — strong and forceful

courage (KUHR-ij) — bravery in times of difficulty or danger

rookie (RUK-ee) — a first-year player or athlete

routine (roo-TEEN) — a regular pattern of movements during a performance

savory (SAY-vur-ee) — food that is salty or spicy rather than sweet

translate (TRANS-late) — to change one language into a different one

veteran (VET-ur-uhn) — a person who has lots of experience in a particular area

Discussion Questions

1. In your own words, discuss how money influenced the events that were happening in Tam's life. How did this issue make Tam feel? What in the text makes you think that?

2. Maren and some of the other cheerleaders are really mean to Tam! What are some of the things they do to Tam? What are some good ways to handle bullies?

3. How does Tam feel at the end of the story? Why? Talk about how her feelings changed throughout the story, and be sure to use examples from the text to support your answers.

Writing Prompts

1. When Tam is upset, her mom tries to make her feel better. Is there an adult in your life who helps you when you're feeling bad? Compare that person's actions to things Tam's mom does.

2. Write a paragraph about what kind of squad captain you think Lily would be. How would she act? How would she treat the rest of the squad? Point to examples in the story to support your reasoning.

3. Tam worked hard and practiced on her own because she wanted to improve her cheering skills. Write two to three paragraphs about something that you've worked hard for. How did you practice or prepare? Did you accomplish your goal?

MORE ABOUT CHEERLEADING

Even though cheerleading first started around 1898 at the University of Minnesota, women and girls weren't allowed to officially cheer until 1923. Cheerleading has grown steadily in popularity ever since — and it's become more and more acrobatic.

In the **basket toss**, a group of strong cheerleaders makes a "basket" by interlocking their arms. A cheerleader steps into the basket and is flung into the air.

A **flyer** is the cheerleader who is thrown during the toss. She is usually a smaller person and often does some kind of acrobatic move during the toss.

Cheerleaders pride themselves on their **flexibility**, and splits are one way to show this off. The cheerleader slides down onto the ground with one leg extended straight in front of her and the other leg extended straight back.

A cheerleader has to be very flexible to get both legs straight. Then she straightens her torso and often raises her arms into the air.

Some cheerleaders work on **handsprings**. In this gymnastic move, a cheerleader squats, then jumps up and back at the same time. She springs into the air and reaches her arms toward the ground behind her. She lands on her hands and then flips her body over, landing back on her feet. It's a pretty spectacular move!

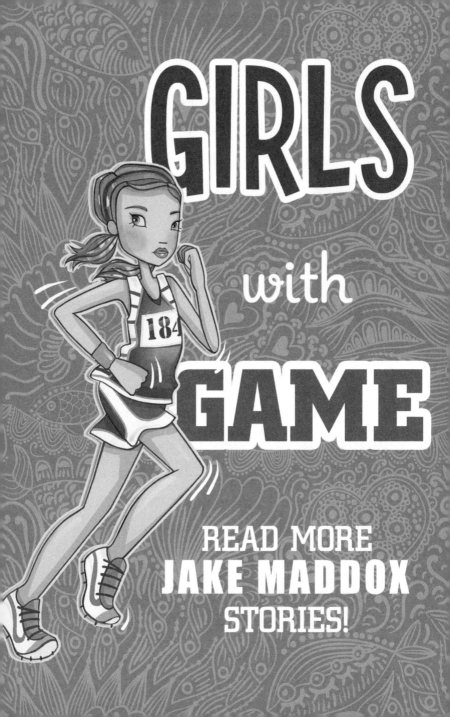

THE FUN DOESN'T STOP HERE!

Discover more:

VIDEOS & CONTESTS
GAMES & PUZZLES
HEROES & VILLAINS
AUTHORS & ILLUSTRATORS

www.capstonekids.com

Find cool websites and more books just like this one at www.facthound.com.
Just type in the book I.D.
9781496549716
and you're ready to go!